JARED CHAPMAN

FRUITS in SUITS

ABRAMS APPLESEED, NEW YORK

THE ART FOR THIS BOOK WAS CREATED DIGITALLY IN A BATHING SUIT, EVEN THOUGH IT WASN'T QUITE BATHING-SUIT SEASON YET. CATALOGING-IN-PUBLICATION DATA HAS BEEN APPLIED FOR AND MAY BE OBTAINED FROM THE LIBRARY OF CONGRESS. ISBN 978-1-4197-2298-1. TEXT AND ILLUSTRATIONS COPYRIGHT © 2017 JARED CHAPMAN. BOOK DESIGN BY CHAD W. BECKERMAN. PUBLISHED IN 2017 BY ABRAMS APPLESEED, AN IMPRINT OF ABRAMS. ALL RIGHTS RESERVED. NO PORTION OF THIS BOOK MAY BE REPRODUCED, STORED IN A RETRIEVAL SYSTEM, OR TRANSMITTED IN ANY FORM OR BY ANY MEANS, MECHANICAL, ELECTRONIC, PHOTOCOPYING, RECORDING, OR OTHERWISE, WITHOUT WRITTEN PERMISSION FROM THE PUBLISHER. ABRAMS APPLESEED IS A REGISTERED TRADEMARK OF HARRY N. ABRAMS, INC. FOR BULK DISCOUNT INQUIRIES, CONTACT SPECIALSALES@ABRAMSBOOKS.COM. PRINTED AND BOUND IN CHINA. 10 9 8 7 6 5 4 3 2 1

ABRAMS The Art of Books
115 West 18th Street, New York, NY 10011
abramsbooks.com

POMEGRANATES

STRAWBERRY

RED APPLE

CHERRY

PEAR

LIME

PEACH

POOL

FOR LORELEI

SUITS!

I WEAR A SUIT.

YOU WEAR A SUIT.

ONE-PIECE SUITS

AND TWO-PIECE SUITS.

OLD-FASHIONED SUITS

AND MODERN SUITS.

SUITS FOR BABIES

AND SUITS FOR PARENTS.

WAIT A SECOND . . .

SUITS FOR SUNBATHING

AND SUITS FOR THE SHADE.

SIMPLE SUITS

AND SILLY SUITS.

SUITS FOR SCUBA

AND SUITS FOR SURFING.

BUT *I'M* WEARING A SUIT!

IF YOU WANT TO GO SWIMMING, YOU NEED A *SUIT*.

UNLESS . . .

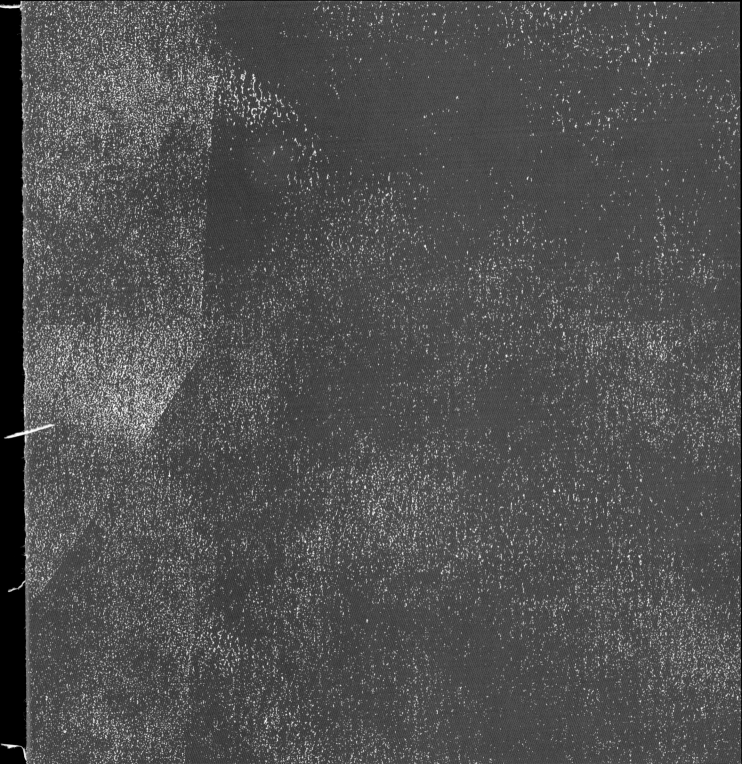

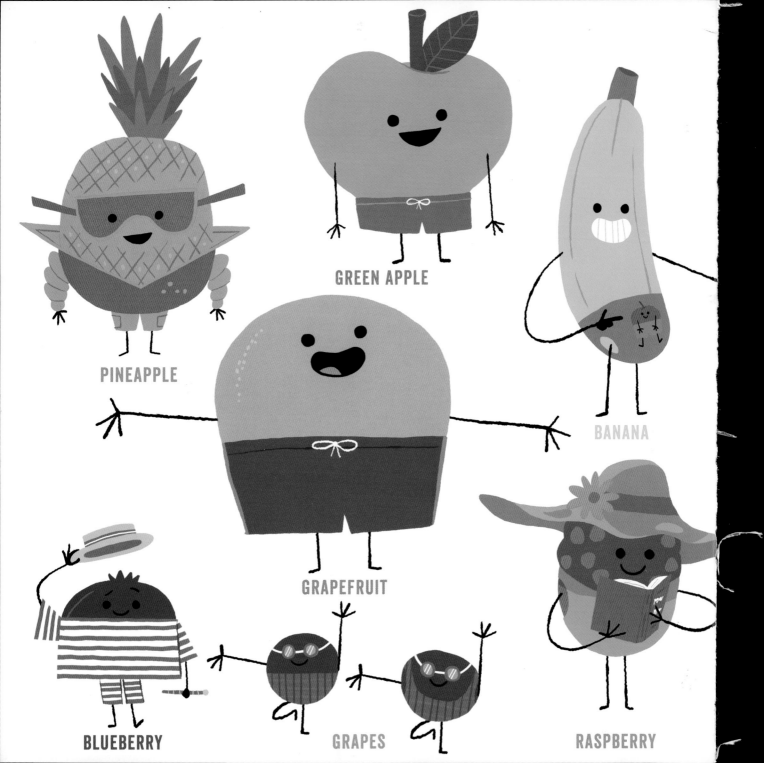

PINEAPPLE

GREEN APPLE

BANANA

GRAPEFRUIT

BLUEBERRY

GRAPES

RASPBERRY